MEET THE GIRL TALK CHARACTERS

Sabrina Wells is petite, with curly auburn hair, sparkling hazel eyes, and a bubbly personality. Sabrina loves magazines, shopping, sleepovers, and most of all, she loves talking to her best friends.

Katie Campbell is a straight-A student and super athlete. With her blond hair, blue eyes, and matching clothes, she's everyone's idea of Little Miss Perfect. But Katie has a few surprises for everyone, including herself!

Randy Zak has just moved to Acorn Falls from New York City, and is she ever cool! With her radical spiked haircut and her hip New York clothes, Randy teaches everyone just how much fun it is to be different.

Allison Cloud is a Native American Indian. Allison's supersmart and really beautiful. But she has one major problem: She's thirteen years old, five foot seven, and still growing!

KATIE AND SABRINA'S BIG COMPETITION

By L. E. Blair

GIRL TALK® series created by Western Publishing Company, Inc.

Western Publishing Company, Inc., Racine, Wisconsin 53404

A MCMXCII

Text by Crystal Johnson

Chapter One

"Hey, Sabs. What's up?" I asked, seeing my best friend, Sabrina Wells, walk toward the locker we share. My name's Katie Campbell. Sabrina and I are in the seventh grade at Bradley Junior High School.

Sabs was wearing a pink down jacket, bright blue leggings, and yellow high-top sneakers, not to mention that her curly hair is a deep red color. I was thinking that she looked really nice — kind of like a rainbow — so I guess I didn't notice the way she was walking at first.

"Katie!" Sabs groaned. "I think I'm going to fall over!"

That was when I noticed that she was limping. "Sabs! What's wrong?" I cried, running over to help her. "Did you sprain your ankle on the way to school?"

"It's worse than that," Sabs said, making a face. "I tried out a new exercise video last night, and now I can't walk! My muscles are really sore." She was kind of leaning to one side, so she looked even shorter than usual — which is only four feet ten and three-quarters inches to start with!

I wrinkled my nose and sniffed as Sabrina leaned on the locker right next to ours. She smelled minty and medicine-like, kind of like the way the locker room smells after a hockey game.

"Sabs, did you put on some kind of sports cream?" I asked her.

"Don't tell me you can smell it? Ohmygosh! That's awful!" Sabs exclaimed, looking horrified. "I got it from Luke. He said it would make my muscles stop hurting, so I rubbed it in this morning after I took a hot bath."

"You didn't!" I said. I knew from experience what must have happened.

Sabs nodded dejectedly. "I rubbed it into the back of my legs, and then all of a sudden it felt like my skin was on fire! I tried washing it off, but that didn't help at all!"

"Sabs, after a bath is the worst time to use

that stuff. Your pores are all open, so your skin absorbs more of it, and that makes it sting like crazy," I explained.

"Well, Luke didn't tell me that," Sabs said. "And now, on top of the stinging, I have to go around smelling like a wintergreen mint all day!"

I couldn't help giggling a little, until I saw how upset Sabs looked. "It's not so bad, Sabs," I lied, trying to make her feel better. "Really."

Sabs tried to bend over to reach her books at the bottom of the locker, but she couldn't get her hand down past her knees.

"Here, I'll get your math book for you." I knew that was her first class. I stared hopelessly at her half of the locker. It was a jumbled heap. "Where is it?" I finally asked.

"It's the one right under my gym shoes. No, under the pink notebook. That's it!" she said triumphantly as I touched the right book.

I pulled the textbook out slowly, holding my breath and hoping I wouldn't start an avalanche.

One major difference between Sabs and me is that I am totally organized and neat, while she tends to be — well, scattered. She always seems to be running in about a million different directions at once.

Grinning, I handed Sabs the book. Since I was already squatting down, I retied the laces on my new leather shoe-boots.

"Hey, guys!" I looked up to see our two other best friends, Randy Zak and Allison Cloud, standing over us. Randy was wearing tinted granny glasses. Not that she has bad eyesight or anything — the lenses were just plain glass. But they looked cool with her black zip-up turtleneck, zebra-striped miniskirt, black leggings, and black granny boots.

Anyway, Randy was staring at Sabs over the top of her glasses. "What's going on, Sabs?" she asked. "You look like you're trying to do one of those robot dances or something."

"Are you okay?" Al added, holding her books under one arm.

Sabs was making jerky movements as she tried to get her coat off. "Ow!" she said after reaching one arm over to pull at her other sleeve.

"Your arms hurt, too?" I asked.

Randy and Al exchanged a look. "What's going on?" Randy asked.

"Sabs overdid it last night with her new

exercise tape," I explained.

"It comes in two parts," Sabs added. "One for beginners and one for advanced. I thought since I was kind of in the middle, I would do both workouts."

Al's eyes widened. "I don't think that's how it works, Sabs," she said, shaking her head. Her long, straight dark hair was held off her face by a burnt-orange headband. She also had on a yellow-and-burnt-orange-striped cotton shirt and jeans with a patterned orange flannel lining turned up at the bottoms.

"Well, the instructions said to make it burn!" Sabs said. Then she giggled and added, "I guess that's exactly what I did when I used that smelly sports creme."

"Did you ever get sore muscles when you were working out for the hockey team?" Al asked, turning to me.

"Definitely. Especially at first," I said, remembering how my muscles had ached when I was trying out for the team. "But I've always skated, so it wasn't like I was using new muscles or anything. Besides, Coach Budd always made sure we started out slow and warmed up really well. When your muscles are cold or tired, you can get hurt."

Sabs had finally taken off her coat and was gingerly stretching her arm out to hang the coat on a hook in our locker. Suddenly she paused and looked at us with an excited expression on her face.

"Hey! Why don't you guys come over after school today?" she suggested. "We could do the exercise video together. It'll be a lot more fun that way."

"What about your sore muscles?" Allison asked, looking dubious.

"Well, Luke said I have to work out the pain," Sabs told us. Luke is Sabs's older brother — or one of them. She actually has four, including her twin, Sam.

"Well, I think that you should just work on walking for now!" Randy said. "Besides, I'm not really into working out in front of a TV screen. I'd much rather go skateboarding outside in the fresh air."

Actually, I agreed with Randy. I could understand wanting to be in good shape. But I'd rather go skating or swimming or biking instead of doing exercises to a video.

I didn't want to hurt Sabs's feelings, but I

had something to do after school. "I can't come over, either. I promised Michel I'd go to the sporting goods store at the mall with him after school today. He needs new sneakers," I told Sabrina.

Michel Beauvais is my stepbrother. A few months ago my mom married Michel's father, Jean-Paul. At first it was strange to have a stepfather and stepbrother, but now I think they're really cool. I guess it sounds sort of corny, but I'm really beginning to feel like my mother, my older sister, Emily, Michel, Jean-Paul, and I are one big family.

"I have to check out the sports store, too, if I'm going to get in shape," Sabs said. "I'll definitely be able to work out better if I get some of those Lycra exercise pants. You know, the ones with the neon colors all over them."

Randy, Al, and I looked at each other and started cracking up.

"Sabs, I don't think those exercise pants will make a difference," I said. "It's what you do that's important, not what you wear."

"I know, but I always do better when I look good," she said. "Well, what if we all go to the mall with you and Michel this afternoon?"

"Definitely," I agreed. Having my friends there would really make the trip a lot more fun. We usually have a great time hanging out there together.

"Count me in," Randy said. "I need to get some new wheels for my board."

"I'll come, too," Al agreed with a smile. "I want to check out the baby store and see if I can get something for Barrett and Charlie." She shifted her schoolbooks to her hip and added, "These days I can't get anything for Barrett without bringing Charlie something, too." Allison has a seven-year-old brother named Charlie and a new baby sister named Barrett.

Randy looked at all of us over the top of her granny glasses. "Maybe we can even catch a movie! It is Friday, after all."

"Sounds good to me!" I said.

Just then the warning bell rang. I grabbed my own books for first-period class, then shut the locker door. "Well, better go," I said. "See you guys third period for English!"

I smiled to myself as I hurried down the hall to class. Sometimes having friends like Sabs and Al and Randy made me feel great.

Chapter Two

"Bonjour!" Michel said cheerfully, stepping up to my locker. School was finally over and Randy, Al, Sabs, and I were all waiting with our coats on. "What's up?"

Michel's dark eyes crinkled at the corners as he smiled at us. He was dressed in his favorite polo shirt, faded jeans, and old high-top sneakers, which were starting to get holes in them.

"Hi, Michel," Sabs said, smiling at him. "We're going to the mall with you and Katie."

Michel looked at the four of us. Then he ran a hand through his short brown hair and glanced up and down the hallway. He didn't look too crazy about the idea of going to the mall with four girls.

His eyes lit up as he saw Sam, Sabs's twin, who also happens to be friends with Michel. Sam was walking down the hall toward us with his friends Nick Robbins, Jason McKee, and Arizonna Blake.

"Hey, guys, hold on a second!" Michel cried, running over to them. I couldn't hear the rest of what he said, but a second later the whole group came up to where my friends and I were.

"Shopping with my sister on purpose?" Sam was saying, eyeing Sabs skeptically. "I don't know, Michel. I mean, you and I are friends, but this is asking a lot!"

Sabs faced him with her hands on her hips. "So don't come, Sam. That'd be fine with me!"

"That'd be fine with you?" he repeated, mimicking Sabs's voice perfectly. He looks a lot like Sabs, too, with red hair and a freckled nose that he was wrinkling at her. "In that case, we'll definitely come," he said to Michel.

Of course, Michel and the other guys started cracking up, which only made Sabs madder. "Stop it!" she said, stamping her foot. She turned to me and asked, "Can all of us fit in Mrs. Smith's car?" Mrs. Smith is our house-keeper, and she picks Michel and me up after school almost every day. She is really nice about it and picks us up from Fitzie's or any of our friends' homes, too.

"No problem," Michel said quickly, before I could answer. "We've done it before." Obviously he really wanted his friends to come along.

"But we end up feeling like sardines when we do," I put in.

The guys didn't seem to care about that, though. "So we'll go," Sam said, giving Sabs this smug look.

Michel turned to Arizonna, Jason, and Nick. "You're coming, too, right?" he asked.

"Sure," Arizonna replied. He tapped the neon-striped skateboard that was tucked under his arm. "I need to check out some new wheels for my board."

"You, too? Cool!" said Randy. "We can head over to Radical Riders together." She taught Arizonna how to skateboard right after he moved here from California. Now both of them go skateboarding all the time.

"We'll come, too," Nick said, giving Jason a kidding shove. The next thing I knew, all the guys were shoving each other around, laughing, as they went down the hall ahead of us. Sometimes guys are *really* weird.

"I feel like a pretzel!" Al said after we had

piled out of Mrs. Smith's car in front of the Widmere Mall. Al is five feet seven and still growing, so being crammed in that car couldn't have been very comfortable for her.

Sabs waved to Mrs. Smith as she drove off. "That must be some sort of record," Sabs said, with a laugh. "Nine kids plus Mrs. Smith in a regular sedan!"

As we walked onto the main concourse, I saw that the restaurants and snack bars that filled this level were really packed. "It's probably just because this is the floor with all the eating places," I said. "The stores probably won't be so bad."

We pushed our way through the crowds toward the escalator to the downstairs level, where McLaughlin's Sporting Goods was.

"This floor is packed, too," Sabs said, leaning over the edge of the escalator and looking down.

"Yeah. And check out McLaughlin's! It's a madhouse!" Randy exclaimed.

I looked down and to the right, where I knew the store was located. There was actually a crowd of people waiting outside the store to get in. I couldn't believe it!

"This is crazy," Sabs said, frowning. "Is there a sale? Is it some president's birthday or something?"

Al shook her head. "Not that I know of."

I spotted the guys outside McLaughlin's now. They were trying to push their way into the store, but they weren't making much headway.

"The other stores don't seem to be half as packed," Randy commented. "What's the big deal there?"

She was right. Just about everyone getting off the escalator was going right to McLaughlin's. "We might as well go find out," I said.

It took us almost twenty minutes to push our way into the store. Right inside the door we found ourselves squashed next to a display of sports socks by the checkout counter. Behind the counter was a harried-looking guy with blond hair and a green knit shirt that said McLAUGHLIN'S on it.

"Excuse me! What's going on?" I asked loudly. It was pretty noisy in there, and I wanted to make sure he heard me.

"You don't know?" the clerk said, looking surprised. "It's the promotion for the grand opening of the new sports complex on the edge of town. It's been advertised on the radio for days. We're giving away free one-day passes and T-shirts."

He gestured toward the rear of the store and added, "The D.J. from KZAP is here. And there's a promoter from the complex signing up kids for a big triathlon being held there in three weeks."

"Wow, I can't believe we haven't heard about this," Sabs said as she was jostled by the crowd.

Al bit her lip thoughtfully. "I remember reading about the sports complex. It's supposed to be huge! They've built an Olympic-size pool, a half-mile track, racquetball courts, tennis courts, a basketball court, weight rooms — and it's all indoors."

Randy nodded, looking impressed. "That's more sports than even you could handle, Katie!"

I giggled and pushed ahead through the crowd, trying to get to the section where the exercise clothes were kept. Since Michel's friends were with him, I didn't think he would need my help picking out sneakers anymore.

At this point I just wanted Sabs to get her exercise clothes and for us to get out of there.

Looking up, I saw a poster for the IronKids Triathlon hanging on the wall. I couldn't resist stopping to read it.

"What's that?" Sabs asked, stopping next to me.

"It's a poster for that triathlon event the clerk told us about," I answered, still scanning the print. "It's called the Ironkids Triathlon and it's going to be held at the new Acorn Falls Sports Complex three weeks from tomorrow. It sounds really cool!"

I began to read the interesting parts off to Sabs. "It's for kids ages seven to fourteen. They'll be broken down into two groups — Juniors, who are seven-to-ten-year-olds, and Seniors, who are eleven-to-fourteen-year-olds. There's going to be a girl winner and a boy winner for both groups, and the prize for first place is a one-year membership to the sports complex!"

"Do you think you want to enter?" Al asked, speaking up from behind me. "What would you have to do?"

"There's a 200-meter swim, a 6-mile bike

ride, and a 1.2-mile run," I replied. I could feel myself getting really excited as I looked at my friends. "Doesn't that sound great? I can do all those things. I'm going to sign up!"

"I'll sign up, too!" Sabs chimed in. "That way we can do it together. It'll be really fun!"

I looked at her in complete surprise. I definitely wouldn't have thought this was the kind of thing Sabs would be interested in. I mean, she's not into serious sports or anything. She must not have understood how difficult it would be.

"Sabs, do you realize how hard it is to swim 200 meters, bike 6 miles, and run 1.2 miles?" I asked skeptically.

Sabs's brow furrowed in concentration. "Well, I'm not really sure how long 200 meters is, but I think it would be fun to try," she answered. "Don't you?"

Fun wasn't exactly a word that came to mind when I thought about training. It was definitely challenging, and satisfying, though. Maybe that was what Sabs meant.

"It's going to take a lot of hard work and training," I told her. "I mean, the triathlon is the hardest event you can participate in!" I didn't want to scare her or anything, but I wanted to make sure she knew what she was getting into.

"So you don't want to do it anymore?" Sabs asked, looking disappointed.

"I still want to do it," I said quickly.

"Well, then I want to do it, too," she said emphatically. "We can train together! My muscles are already feeling better since this morning, and I really want to keep up this working-out stuff. It'll be fun, Katie, you'll see. Now let's go over and check out those new neon workout clothes."

I followed quietly as she pulled me toward the racks of workout clothes. Sabs was probably right. It would be fun training for the triathlon with a partner

So then why was there a niggling doubt in the back of my mind?

Chapter Three

"Did you guys see the cool T-shirts Katie and I got when we signed up for the triathlon?" Sabrina asked when we settled into a booth at the Pizza Paradise on the mall's main concourse.

"They're really nice," Al said.

The T-shirt was white with blue writing on it that said FIRST ANNUAL IRONKIDS TRIATHLON in big letters. Below the letters were stylized silhouettes of three athletes — one swimming, one biking, and one running. A small logo on the pocket showed that the triathlon was being sponsored by the Acorn Falls Sports Complex.

I thought the shirts looked great, too. I couldn't wait to wear mine when I ran the race. But for now all I could think about was the pepperoni pizza we had just ordered.

It had taken forever for Michel to pick out a pair of sneakers he liked, and for Sabs to get some exercise clothes. I was really relieved when we finally left the store and I could start breathing again. Now I was really hungry!

I reached past Sam to take a slice of pizza. That was when I noticed that he was staring across the table at Sabs with a look of total disbelief on his face. "A triathlon!" he said. "Are you crazy?"

"Hey! What's that supposed to mean?" I said defensively.

Sabs glared over the table at her twin. "Yeah! Don't you think that Katie and I can do it?"

"I think that Katie can do it. It's you I'm worried about," Sam told her.

"I'll have you know that I do fifty sit-ups and a hundred leg lifts every night before bed!" Sabs shot back.

"Ooooh!" Sam said, looking at the other guys. "Well, when they have a triathlon for sit-ups and leg lifts, you'll be all set."

All of the guys started to laugh, which made me kind of mad. I was pretty surprised that Sabs wanted to enter the triathlon, too. But I also thought that as long as she had made that decision, we should all support her. I knew I'd be really mad if anyone treated me the way Sam was treating Sabs right then.

Allison spoke up. "Well, I think it's great that Sabrina wants to do this."

Randy finished chewing a bite of pizza, then took a long drink of her soda. "Me too. You guys are just proving once again that you cannot handle it when girls are just as good at sports as you are," she said. "It's the same thing you guys did when Katie decided to try out for the hockey team."

The guys all looked a little embarrassed. They had given me a hard time, but I showed them. By the end of the hockey season, I was the second-highest scorer on the team.

"Why don't *you guys* sign up for the triathlon?" I said, shooting them a challenging look. "Then you could show us girls how it's done!"

Michel held up his hands defensively. "Hey, don't get mad at me!" he said, talking through a mouthful of pizza. It was totally gross. "I think you will both do great, but I sure don't want to swim, bike, and then run!"

My friends and I all looked at the other guys.

"I'm with Michel," Arizonna said quickly. "I bet you'll do great, Sabrina."

Nick and Jason backed down, too. The only one who didn't say anything was Sam.

"How about you, Samuel?" Sabs challenged. I knew she was really mad at him, since she was using his full name. "You're awfully quiet — for the first time in your life!"

We all just stared at Sam. After the way he'd just insulted Sabs, there was no way we were going to let him off the hook!

Sam's freckled face got bright red. "I, uh, I don't think I have to prove anything," he mumbled. "Besides, I never said I could do all that."

"So you admit Sabs and Katie are better athletes than you are," Randy said.

Sam looked like he was about to give in — until he saw the satisfied look on Sabs's face.

"I didn't say that! I just said that I didn't think that Sabs could do a triathlon," he blurted out, making a face at her. "And she'll prove that all by herself!"

Without even thinking, I jumped to my feet, practically knocking over Nick, who was next to me. "Well, you guys will all see!" I said. "Sabs and I are going to be the first two girls to cross the finish line!"

I was really mad at Sam for not having more faith in Sabs. "We're going to start training tomorrow," I went on. "And in three weeks you guys had better be waiting at the finish line to congratulate us!"

I caught the uncertain look on Sabrina's face. But then she said to the guys, "Yeah! You just wait and see!"

The next afternoon I sat at my desk in my room waiting for my friends to arrive for a sleepover. We had decided the day before at the pizza shop to have a sleepover over today. Suddenly I heard Al call out, "Hi, Katie! We're here!" Soon she and Randy and Sabs came tramping into my room.

"Sorry we're late," Sabs added. "I had to wait for my dad to come back from doing the grocery shopping before he could drive us over."

I jumped up from my desk and ran over to help my friends stack their bags by the door. "I was dying for you guys to get here!" I told them. "The cook made sugar cookies for us and everything."

Pretty soon we all had our shoes off and were sitting around my room, munching on the plate of cookies that I had put on the carpet.

I happen to think that my room is a really comfortable place to hang out in. It's decorated in my favorite colors, pink and blue. It's also got thick carpeting, plus pretty oversize throw pillows and a big canopy bed.

"Katie, I'm proud of how you stood up to those guys yesterday," Randy said, leaning against the foot of my bed and munching on a sugar cookie.

Al was standing by my bookcase, looking through the books and magazines I had put there. She turned to me. "Yeah, you really put them in their place," she agreed.

"You really were great, Katie," Sabs added, but I noticed that she didn't sound as enthusiastic as Al and Randy.

Sabs hesitated, biting her lip. "Do you really think that we can be the first two girls to finish?"

So she *was* a little worried about it after all. She didn't think she could really come in first. I was about to tell her not to worry, that it didn't matter if she came in first or last. What really counted was that she was going to enter the competition and do her best. But then I remembered what Coach Budd always told us about how the only way to be a winner was to believe in yourself. Maybe all Sabs needed was for us to have faith in her.

"Sure! I think we can really do it," I said enthusiastically. "Just because Sam doesn't believe in you doesn't mean that he's right, Sabs."

Sabs looked at me. "Really? You really think I can do it?" she asked.

"Definitely," Randy, Al, and I all said at the same time.

"I hope you're right," Sabs said. "I mean, Sam will never let me live it down if we don't win after you told him we would."

She kind of mumbled the last part and looked quickly down at the magazine she'd been flipping through on my bed. I could tell she was feeling doubtful again.

"Listen, all we have to do is train really hard," I said, trying to get her into this again. "We have to have a strategy."

Sabs brightened. "That sounds good. Like when Sam and I ran for president and vice president of the seventh grade."

"And your strategy that time was a total success," Al put in optimistically.

Jumping up, I ran across my bedroom to my desk and grabbed the notebook I had been writing in when my friends arrived. Then I sat down on my bed next to Sabs.

"What's that?" Sabrina asked, pointing at the notebook.

"Our training schedule — or it will be anyway," I told her. "I started mapping out the next three weeks day by day. I figured out exactly how many miles we have to swim, bike, and run every day in order to be in top shape for the triathlon. First you have to tell me if there are any days that you can't work out."

Sabrina looked at the paper with a frown. "You mean we have to do *all* this stuff every day for three weeks? Don't you think it's kind of a lot, Katie?"

I took another look at the schedule, but I really didn't see anything we could cut out. Still, it probably looked like a lot to Sabs, since she wasn't used to rigorous training.

"We don't have to do all three things every day," I explained. "But we have to do at least one of them every day. And we should work out with weights to strengthen our muscles, too."

"Um, okay. I guess so," Sabs said, still looking at the sheet. "But I can't work out on Sundays, because my mom likes us all to be home for our big family meal in the afternoon and I have to help with the dishes afterward. Oh — and Tuesday is my day to help with dinner, and I can't do anything on Saturdays until all my chores are done."

Well, that wasn't great news, but I figured we could work around it. I still planned on working out every day, but I wanted to make sure that Sabs got in enough training so that she would be in shape, too.

"I guess we'll have to work extra hard the other days. And then we have to pick a day to go down to the sports complex and see the layout of the course," I said, thinking out loud. "We're allowed to use the facilities, since we signed up for the triathlon."

I bit on the end of my pencil, trying to figure out the best day to go to the complex.

"Katie, do we have to do this now?" Sabs said, breaking into my thoughts. "I mean, it's a slumber party. We're supposed to do fun things."

"Oh — sorry, guys," I said, feeling embarrassed. "When it comes to sports, I really get into what I'm doing. I guess I forget that it's not so interesting to other people." I closed my notebook. "Let's do something else. Sabs and I can figure out our training schedule on the phone tomorrow."

"Great! Let's all take the romance quiz in this month's *Young Chic*!" Sabrina said, holding up her magazine.

What I really wanted to do was go down to our exercise room in the basement, but I knew that would be rude. There was still plenty of time to set up our training schedule. Besides, I didn't want Sabs to get totally discouraged before we even started.

Stifling a tiny feeling of disappointment, I lay on the carpet, hugging a pillow to my chest. "Okay, Sabs. What's the first question?"

Chapter Four

When I woke up for school on Monday morning, the first thing I heard was the sound of sleet hitting my bedroom window.

"Oh, no!" I cried, jumping out of bed. I ran over to my window seat and looked out between the pink-and-white-striped curtains.

This was definitely bad news. I went to my desk and took down the training schedule I had pinned to my bulletin board. I had planned for Sabs and me to go bike riding after school today. But if this sleet didn't stop, we'd have to change our plans. Sabs couldn't work out on Tuesday, so on Wednesday we would have to go bike riding *and* running. Well, today we'd just do the weight lifting that I'd planned to do on Wednesday.

I had marked a calendar to show what Sabs and I were supposed to train for every day. I decided that when we each finished training for a particular day, I would put check marks next to our names, using colored pencils. When Sabs and I had worked out the schedule the night before on the phone, we had decided to use pink for her and blue for me.

After my friends had left yesterday, I had begun working out by myself in our exercise room in the basement. I lifted some weights, used the rowing machine, and then did twenty laps in our pool. It was really great having everything I needed to train right in my own house.

I thought I might have a chance of coming in first in the triathlon if I really worked hard. I decided to do everything I could to try to win. It made me feel good to see that there were already some blue check marks next to my name.

Actually, it was kind of good that Sabs hadn't worked out with me, because it gave me a chance to fine-tune our training schedule. I wrote down exactly how many repetitions we should do with each weight and how many minutes and miles to do on the treadmill and rowing machine.

"Yikes!" I said, glancing at the alarm clock

on my nightstand. I had totally lost track of time, and now it was after seven-thirty. I had to leave for school in less than half an hour. Jumping up, I ran to the bathroom that connects my room with Michel's room. I wanted to get into the shower before he got a chance to hog the bathroom!

Luckily, I don't take a long time in the shower. Ten minutes later I was back in my room drying my hair. Then I went into my walk-in closet to look at my clothes. Because of the weather, I didn't want to wear a skirt and good shoes, so I pulled out a pair of dark green wool pants that had leather suspenders on them. Mom had bought them for me along with a soft cream-colored wool shirt that had a green floral print on the collar and cuffs. I put them both on, along with cream-colored wool socks, a dark green velvet headband, and my flat brown leather boots.

I was just zipping my books neatly into my leather backpack when I heard Michel stumbling into the shower. That meant that I would have time at least to have a glass of orange juice before we left.

I looked out the window one more time,

hoping that the sleet had stopped, but it had only turned to rain. Sometimes I missed being able to walk to school, the way I used to before we moved to our new house. But our new neighborhood is pretty far from school. And I had to admit that on days like today I was really glad that we got a ride.

Slinging my backpack over one shoulder, I went down the back stairs to the kitchen. A pitcher of juice and some warm muffins were set out on the kitchen table for breakfast. The muffins looked really good, and I bit into a blueberry crumb one right away.

No one else was around, so I figured that Mom and Jean-Paul must already have left for work. My sister, Emily, usually drives us to school but she had an early cheerleading meeting at the high school, so Mrs. Smith was driving Michel and me today instead.

I looked up as Michel came stampeding down the back stairs and flew out of the stairway into the kitchen. He was holding his books under his left arm, and they were sticking out in different directions. I was sure they were going to go flying, but they didn't.

"Good morning, K.C. Great, there are

muffins!" he cried and shoved one in his mouth before he even sat down. His books clunked down on the table.

I frowned, noticing that his hair was still totally wet and dripping. "Michel, aren't you going to dry your hair?"

"Why should I bother?" He poured some juice and gulped it down. "It's raining outside anyway. It will just get wet again."

He was acting like that was the most logical explanation in the world. In a way, I guess he had a point, so I just shrugged and went back to eating my muffin.

"So, are you and Sabrina going to work out for the triathlon today?" Michel asked.

I looked at him closely to see if he was sincere or if he was just teasing us for signing up for the triathlon, the way Sam had.

He looked pretty serious, so I answered, "I wanted to go bike riding outside today, but now it's pouring. I guess we'll have to work out in the pool and the weight room."

I hadn't wanted to do that again today, since that was what I had done yesterday. I liked to work different muscles in each training session so that the muscles I worked one day would have a chance to rest.

"Why don't you go to the new sports complex and check out things there?" Michel suggested. "You could run on the indoor track."

"That's a great idea!" I cried. I couldn't believe that I hadn't thought of it myself. Sabs and I had planned to go to the sports complex next week anyway to see the track and the pool and the layout of the course for the triathlon. Now that I thought about it, working out on the actual course would be a really great way to train — especially since there was no way we could be outside today.

I kept thinking about the new plan while Mrs. Smith drove Michel and me to school. I couldn't wait to tell Sabs about it! Once we got there, I hurried through the halls, which were packed with kids in their wet raincoats. When I got to our locker, Sabs wasn't there yet, so I hung my raincoat up and waited for her.

Sabs is not exactly known for her promptness. In fact, she's usually lucky if she gets to school before the late bell rings! Normally it doesn't bother me — I mean, that's just part of Sabs's style. But today I really wanted to see her so I could tell her about working out later.

"Boy! It's raining cats and dogs out there!" Sabs said as she appeared around the corner. Her yellow raincoat and umbrella were dripping water all over the hall. "I wonder where that expression comes from anyway?"

I laughed, picturing a bunch of cats and dogs falling out of the sky. "It is kind of silly," I agreed. "Listen, Sabs, I've got great news about today's workout!"

"Workout?" Sabs echoed, looking doubtful. "You mean you still want to go bike riding? But it's pouring!" she said, peeling off her raincoat and hanging it in our locker. A stream of water dripped all over her books, but she didn't seem to care.

"Sabs, we have to train as much as possible if we want to win," I said, trying to make her understand.

"Katie, you're not going to make us ride bikes in the rain, are you?" Sabs pleaded.

"No, of course not. That wouldn't be safe. But here's the good part. Mrs. Smith is going to drive us over to the sports complex so we can practice running on the new indoor track!" I said in an excited rush. "I think there are even bikes we can use on the track. Isn't that great?"

"Cool!" Sabs exclaimed. "The complex is supposed to be awesome. And I've never ridden a bike on an indoor track before. I bet it will be really fun!"

One great thing about Sabs is that she's always up for something new. At least now she seemed enthusiastic about working out.

"Let's see," Sabs continued. "I'll have to get my running shoes from home, and I'll wear my new Lycra pants that I bought at the mall Friday. And maybe I'll wear my triathlon T-shirt — or should I save that and wear it for the first time at the triathlon?"

I shook my head at her. I was really glad that she was getting excited about training for the triathlon. I just wished she was more interested in the sports part of it — and not only in what workout clothes she was going to wear!

Chapter Five

The icy rain was still pouring down when Mrs. Smith pulled up in front of Bradley after school. In spite of the weather I was totally psyched for today's workout. I'd hardly paid attention in any of my classes because I kept thinking about what the sports complex would be like. Now all we had to do was stop by Sabrina's house so she and I could change, and then we would be there! I was really glad to see that Mrs. Smith had remembered to bring my nylon duffel bag with all of my workout clothes.

"We'll be right back," I told Mrs. Smith when we got to the Wellses'. Then Sabs and I made a dash for her front door.

After leaving our raincoats in the closet, we ran up the stairs to Sabs's room, which is up in the attic. Sitting down on her bed, I opened up the duffel bag. I pulled out my running shoes, a

36

pair of gray sweatpants, a white pocket T-shirt, and white sweat socks.

"Great! Mrs. Smith even remembered to pack a rubber band for my hair and a towel," I said, looking at the things that were still in my bag.

"She really is great, Katie. I mean, she drives us everywhere and she's always smiling and so friendly. I'd trade all four of my brothers for just one of her!" Sabs said, giggling. I knew she didn't really mean that about her brothers, but it was still nice to know that she liked Mrs. Smith.

I quickly changed into my clothes and sat back on the bed. Meanwhile, Sabs was pulling clothes out of her drawers and flinging them on the floor. "I know I have a T-shirt that matches the purple stripe in my new exercise pants!" she mumbled while she searched.

"I think that yellow T-shirt would look good, too, Sabs," I said, pointing to a yellow spot in the pile. "It matches the yellow squiggles on the pants."

"You're right! I'll wear that one," she said, plucking it out. "Now I just have to find my yellow socks," she said.

I almost groaned when Sabs pulled open a drawer full of loose mismatched socks and started rummaging through it. According to Sabs's clock radio, it was already three-thirty. At this rate, we'd only have an hour to work out before we had to be home for dinner!

"Aha! Found them. Now, where are my sneakers?" Sabs glanced around, frowning.

That I could help with. Jumping off the bed, I ran over to a heap of T-shirts and pawed through until I felt the sneakers underneath. "I saw them here before," I explained, pulling them out. "Okay, let's go!"

"Wait! I need to put my hair up," Sabs said.

I sighed while she went over to her mirror. This wasn't exactly how I had planned our first day of training together.

"Okay?" I asked hopefully as she finished pulling her curls up into a high ponytail with a purple scrunchy.

"Okay!" she cried.

While I grabbed my bag, she ran past me down the stairs. When I caught up with her, she was running in place in the foyer.

"I'm warming up," she explained, grinning at me.

"You're really into this! That's great, Sabs," I said, laughing. "But I thought we'd warm up at the arena. I have a whole series of stretches from hockey practice. I'll teach them to you."

"Cool!" Sabs said. With that, she grabbed her raincoat and was out the door.

It didn't take long before we were pulling up in front of the Acorn Falls Sports Complex.

"Wow!" Sabs gasped as she looked at the shiny new building through the car window.

It was huge! From the outside it looked like an enormous circle made of green-tinted glass and steel supports. "It looks really space-age," I said. "Like something that landed here from another planet or something. I love it!"

"It certainly is impressive," Mrs. Smith agreed.

Sabs's mother was going to pick us up, so we said thank you and good-bye to Mrs. Smith. I was feeling more and more excited as we ran up to the front doors of the complex. I couldn't wait to see all the stuff inside!

As soon as we stepped through the front doors, Sabs stopped short. "This place is amazing!" she cried.

We were in a big open reception area.

Through an archway, I could see people working out in an open area on weight machines. Glass and chrome partitions separated it from a maze of other areas, and I could see some people playing tennis in one area, and squash in another.

A sleek reception desk was set against the wall to the right, so we went over to it. It was gray with a red stripe running around it. The colors exactly matched the gray-and-red abstract-design painting on the walls of the entrance area.

"Hi," I said, smiling at the blond-haired woman standing behind the desk. She was wearing a sleek gray sweatsuit with red trim. "We're here to train for the IronKids Triathlon."

The woman smiled back and introduced herself as Joyce Krieger. After checking to make sure our names were on the list of entrants, she gave us a tour of the complex.

She began in the locker rooms. According to Joyce, there were saunas, steam rooms, and a Jacuzzi in both the men's and the women's locker rooms. Of course, we only saw the women's. She assigned each of us a locker where we could keep our stuff.

After that we saw the weight rooms, the racquetball courts, the aerobics class, the basketball court, and the indoor tennis courts. The coolest part was that almost all the walls were glass, so you could watch people playing or working out. There were people in all the areas, but the complex was so big that I couldn't imagine there ever being enough people to make it crowded.

My head was spinning by the time we got to the parts that Sabs and I were most interested in — the pool and the indoor track.

"Check this out!" Sabs said when we entered the huge, open area.

The track was a big oval at the center of the complex, and the Olympic-size pool was in the middle of the oval. There was a sort of rubberized surface around the track where some people were doing stretches. Potted plants and small trees were arranged in a ring around the pool, separating it a little from the track, and there were bleachers along one wall. The coolest part was that the whole room had glass walls and a glass ceiling. That way, you could almost feel like you were really outside.

"This is the coolest place I've ever seen!" I

said to Sabs, looking up at the rain splattering down on the glass roof. "I bet it's great in here when it's sunny."

Finally the tour was over. We thanked Joyce and then went right to the track to begin our workout.

"Okay. First we'll stretch and warm up by walking a lap around the track," I told Sabs.

She didn't say anything, so I looked at her. Sabs was staring at something over my shoulder. "Sabs?"

"Huh?" She looked at me, startled. "Oh — sorry, Katie," she said, blushing.

I turned in the direction she had been looking and saw right away what was so interesting: Max McAllister, eighth-grade hunk, track star, and all-around perfect guy. Or at least that's how most girls at Bradley Junior High felt.

"Isn't he that guy on the varsity track team?" Sabs asked, biting her lip. "The one who wins all the time? What's his name, Mack something?"

"Max McAllister," I answered. "That's him." I didn't know him personally, but I definitely knew who he was.

"He's a total babe," Sabs said in an excited whisper.

I glanced back at Max, who was warming up on the other side of the track. He had shaggy brown hair and dark eyes and was wearing this neon-green tank top with lightweight black shorts. I wasn't sure how Sabs could tell if he was cute or not, since we weren't that close to him. Anyway, we had other things to think about now.

"Let's get started, okay?" I said. "Just do what I do."

"Yeah, okay," Sabs said distractedly. I could tell her head was already in the clouds, but at least she sat on the floor and began stretching her hamstrings like I did.

"Don't bounce, Sabs, you'll hurt your muscles," I corrected her. "Stretch slowly and then hold it for a few seconds."

I guess I shouldn't have been surprised that she wasn't doing the stretches right. Instead of watching me, her eyes kept flickering over to Max.

"Sabs, he definitely knows you're watching him," I whispered, feeling a little annoyed. I wished she would just concentrate on what we were doing.

Max kept looking over at us. He was doing all these wild stretches and kicking his leg over his head. He probably expected us to be totally impressed, even though I personally thought he looked stupid.

"Katie, shouldn't we do some like that?" Sabs asked, still looking in Max's direction.

"No," I answered.

She finally stopped watching him and turned to me. "But why?" she asked.

"Because they're useless stretches, and they look stupid. Besides, they could hurt you if you're not in good shape already," I told her, getting to my feet. "Come on. I think that's enough stretching. Let's start walking. We'll go slow at first and then faster until we're jogging."

We started walking briskly on the track. It felt really good to get moving. My muscles were a little sore after my workout yesterday, but I could feel them stretching and loosening up.

"Hey, look!" Sabs said, grabbing my arm. "Max is starting to run. Look how fast he goes!"

Just then Max came zipping up to us. "Ladies!" he said, flashing us a big smile. Then he was past us.

"Can we start running now?" Sabs asked, following Max's progress with her eyes.

I frowned. Even if Max was the star of Bradley's track team, I didn't think it was so smart of him to start right off running at top speed.

"Not yet," I said. "We're not warmed up yet. It's really important to start slowly if you don't want to hurt yourself."

Sabs didn't look convinced, but she kept walking. I was sort of glad that Max had disappeared in front of us. With him gone, Sabs started looking like she was more interested in what we were doing.

Unfortunately, he reappeared behind us before long. This time he didn't just run by. He slowed down to our pace and started talking.

"So, ladies. It's nice to see such pretty faces around here. I joined the day they opened this complex, but the members so far have been mostly men or older people," he explained. "You know, like my parents' age."

Sabrina's face was turning bright red, I

noticed. But then, she turns red a lot — especially when cute guys talk to her.

Up close, I saw that Max had these really nice slate-blue eyes. He was tall and slim, with a runner's body. He was cute, I had to admit. But he acted like he knew it, and that kind of bugged me.

"I'm Max McAllister," Max continued. Then he looked at us expectantly.

Sabs finally found her voice. "I'm Sabrina Wells, and this is Katie Campbell," she told him.

Max kept looking at us while we walked around the track. "I think I've seen you around Bradley," he said. "But you're not in the eighth grade, are you?"

"We're in seventh," I answered.

"I'm here training for that triathlon in a couple of weeks. Of course, I'm already in shape, but I don't want to take any chances," Max bragged.

Sabs grinned at him. "We've entered the triathlon, too!" she said. "That's why we're here working out."

I looked at her sideways. Right now Sabs was acting more like she was here to flirt!

By now we had gone more than halfway around the track, so I decided we were warmed up enough. "Come on, Sabs. We can start jogging slowly now."

"Great! I'll run with you," Max said. He flashed Sabs a grin, then took off at a fast pace. Sabs ran right after him.

"Sabs, you can't start off that fast!" I called to her. "You have to build up to it and pace yourself!"

Max was way ahead of Sabs, but he slowed down to wait for her. Then the two of them stood there until I caught up. Sabs was already out of breath from just that one sprint.

"Hey, you're that girl on the boys' hockey team, aren't you?" Max said when I reached them. Somehow I didn't like how he said it. He was acting like I was a freak in a circus or something.

"Yeah," I answered a little defensively.

"Oh, that's really great," he said in this totally insincere voice. Then he ignored me.

Turning to Sabs, he said, "I'm captain of the varsity track team. As long as we're both training for the triathlon, I don't see why we can't work out together. Maybe I can give you some pointers on your technique."

My mouth dropped open. This guy had a lot of nerve, coming over here and acting like he knew more than everybody else. Especially when it was obvious to me that he didn't know a thing about training properly. He didn't know about stretching or pacing, and he certainly didn't know anything about Sabs! If he kept her going at the pace he had started, she'd collapse before the first mile!

"Wow! That would be great!" Sabs gushed. "We'd love it if you could help us train and give us some pointers, wouldn't we, Katie?"

She didn't even bother to wait for my answer. Huffing and puffing, she struggled to keep up with Max.

I just stood there in the middle of the track, staring after them.

Chapter Six

"I'm really glad you guys want to work out with Katie and me today," Sabs said. She turned around in the front seat of Mrs. Smith's car to look at Randy and Allison, who were sitting with me in the back. It was Wednesday afternoon, and Mrs. Smith was driving us all to my house.

"No prob! I could use a little workout," Randy said.

"Me too!" Allison chimed in. "I never get as much exercise in the winter as I do in the summer."

Sabs nodded. "Yeah, I guess that's one of the reasons it feels good to be doing all this stuff for the triathlon," she said. "Anyway, it should be fun with all of us working out together."

I looked skeptically at Sabs. "Don't forget that we have to really work today," I reminded her. "Even though the triathlon is in two weeks, we actually don't have much time to get in shape. And since you can't work out on Sundays or Tuesdays, we have to work extra hard the rest of the week."

"You're right, Katie," Sabs insisted. "Don't worry, I'm up for it."

I hoped she meant that. Today was going to be the second day we were training together for the triathlon, and I was kind of worried about it.

Monday's workout at the sports complex hadn't turned out so great, as far as I was concerned. I ran the three miles that we had planned, but Sabs and Max stopped after a mile and a half. If Sabs kept going at this rate, there was no way she'd be able to come in first in the triathlon. I didn't want to discourage her by being so negative about what had already happened, though. I decided just to make sure we both worked extra hard from now on.

I didn't say much during the rest of the ride. I guess that's because I get quiet when something serious is on my mind.

When we got to my house, we all went into the foyer. "We can change into sweats and T-shirts in my room," I said as we hung up our coats. "My sweats are probably going to be short on you, though, Al."

"No sweat," Al said, giggling.

Randy and Allison were going to borrow some of my stuff. Sabs and I had just convinced them to come with us during lunch today, so they hadn't brought anything to change into. Luckily, they were both wearing sneakers, so that wouldn't be a problem.

"See you guys in Katie's room!" Sabs said, taking off up the stairs at a run. Randy, Al, and I shrugged at one another, then ran after her. By the time we had run up the two flights to my room, we were all laughing and out of breath.

"Boy, Katie, this is a workout in itself!" Randy huffed.

Allison laughed as she put her bookbag down. "Really! Maybe you guys should do this for training."

"Actually, stair climbing is really good exercise," Sabs told us. "My workout video said so. I ran up and down the stairs in my house five times yesterday, since I couldn't work out with Katie."

"Really? That's great, Sabs!" I was glad to

hear she was getting into it and working out on her own.

"Yeah. I did it even though Sam made fun of me the whole time," Sabs added, rolling her eyes.

"I bet he was just teasing," Al said. "But it was probably still a pain."

"Anyway, you'll show him when you two finish the triathlon with flying colors!" Randy said.

I could feel a big smile spreading across my face while I rushed around getting sweatpants and T-shirts for Randy and Allison. It was really nice to know that they had so much faith in us.

"You guys will be there at the triathlon, won't you?" Sabs asked, looking at Randy and Al. She was twisting a strand of her red hair nervously in her fingers. Suddenly she didn't look as sure as Randy that we would both finish with flying colors.

"Of course we will!" Al assured us. She took the blue sweatpants and Bradley T-shirt I had just handed her and started to put them on.

"We wouldn't miss it for anything," Randy added.

"Good, because I think I'm starting to get stage fright!" Sabs confided.

"Stage fright?" I asked, looking at her in confusion.

Sabrina nodded. "Yeah, or the sports equivalent of stage fright. Whenever I think about the triathlon, I get butterflies in my stomach. Don't you?"

I thought for a minute. "Well, before a hockey game I get a little nervous and excited. I guess that's kind of what you're talking about. But the minute I hit the ice, I just concentrate on playing," I told her.

"See? So there's nothing to worry about, Sabs," Randy said, tugging the red T-shirt I had lent her over sweats that I'd cut off to be shorts. "You'll probably be fine at the actual race."

"You had stage fright before the school play, and the minute you said your first line, you were fine," Allison added. "Remember?"

Sabs looked from me to Randy to Al. "I guess you're right," she finally said, smiling. "But we better get going. We have to practice, practice, practice!"

I couldn't help laughing at the way she was imitating a play director. "That's the spirit," I told her. "Let's go!"

A few minutes later we were in the gym in the basement of my house. I went over to the wall by the weight-lifting machines where I had taped up our training schedule. So far, Sabs had a pink check next to the running we did on Monday.

"Sabs and I are supposed to do weight lifting today," I said, "but you guys can use any of the other stuff."

Randy stood there looking around for a minute. I didn't think working out was her kind of thing, but she went over to the treadmill and started jogging.

"I think I'll try the exercise bike," Al decided.

Sabs was looking dubiously at all the weight machines. "Where do we start, Katie?" she asked.

I figured I'd better go through the exercises with her until she got the hang of using the machines. Sabs had never done bench presses before, so I showed her how to lie on her back on one of the benches and lift the weights up and down slowly over her chest.

"Eight . . . nine . . . and ten! Okay, Sabs. Now

ten more," I urged.

Sabs turned her head to look at me. "Ten more?" she asked breathlessly, still holding the weights above her head.

She did look kind of tired and sweaty. I almost gave in and switched to something else. But then I changed my mind. I knew that a coach had to be tough to get the best performance possible from the athletes, and that was what I was going to do with Sabs. I owed it to her to help her prove how good an athlete she could really be.

"It's only twenty pounds," I urged her. "You can do it!"

Sabs didn't look too happy to hear that. She frowned and pushed the weights slowly up away from her chest while I stood next to her and counted.

"Boy, Katie. You're tough!" Randy said, looking over at me from the treadmill. The way she said it, I couldn't tell if she meant it as a compliment or not.

"You're doing pretty good yourself, Randy," Al called over. "You've jogged for almost fifteen minutes!" She was still pedaling on the exercise bike, and beads of sweat were beginning to pop out on her forehead.

"Hey! I thought you . . . hated working out . . . inside?" Sabs said to Randy in between breaths.

"Well, I do. Back home in New York City, I used to go running in Central Park with my dad sometimes," she said, still jogging. "But here in Minnesota, where there are only like twelve warm, sunny days a year, you gotta make exceptions!"

Sabs, Randy, and I all started laughing. Moving to Acorn Falls from New York City hadn't been easy for Randy at first.

"Come on, Ran, admit it. Minnesota isn't such a bad place," I said, pretending to be insulted. "You just have to get used to it."

Randy grinned at us. "I'm trying! I mean, here I am in Katie's cellar running on a little machine and going nowhere, and you don't hear me complaining, do you?"

"Well, not exactly," Allison said, cracking up.

Then Sabs let the weights down one last time and said triumphantly, "Ten!"

I frowned down at her. By my count she was only up to seven. "Sabs, that was not ten!"

She sat up on the bench and wiped her sweaty forehead. "Well, it felt like ten," she said firmly. "Anyway, Max McAllister says that lifting weights isn't important for running. He even said that if you build up big muscles, they weigh you down and make you run slower!"

Max McAllister! What did he have to do with our training schedule — the one *Sabs and I* had agreed on? It seemed like every time I turned around at school the last couple of days, he was talking to Sabs and telling her totally wrong things about training. Not only that, but most of the time he was rude to me, even though I had tried to be as nice as possible.

Taking a deep breath, I faced Sabs and put my hands on my hips. "First of all, we're lifting weights to build strength, not muscle," I told her. "We need upper-body strength for the swimming part of the triathlon. Second, we're not going to build big, heavy muscles in three weeks by just lifting twenty pounds forty times every other day! And third, Max McAllister does not know everything!"

Sabs and I just stared at each other. Finally Randy spoke up. "So who is this Max McAllister guy anyway?" she asked. I could tell she was trying to break the tension a little.

"He's the captain of the varsity track team," Sabs said, looking at me like that proved that what he said about running was true.

Al got off the bicycle and went over to the rowing machine. "He came in third in the state in the fifty-yard dash last year," she added.

"You know, Katie," Sabs said, looking down at the bench instead of at me, "I really think we should work out with him next week at the arena. He did offer to help us train."

I tried not to show them all how mad I was that Sabs didn't trust me to be a good trainer. "I thought we agreed on our training schedule last weekend," I said. "It's only Wednesday of our first week of training and already you want to change it? We really don't have a lot of time until the triathlon!"

"I know, but Max is a good runner, and he offered . . ." Sabrina said again. "Besides, I'm sure he's going to win first place of all the boys."

I already knew that Max was counting on his running speed to win it for him. From what he'd told Sabs, he wasn't even really practicing swimming or bike riding. If that was his attitude about the triathlon, then I definitely didn't want his help!

"Yeah? Well, we'll see how he does during the triathlon," I said hotly. I noticed Randy and Al look at each other. I guess I had sounded kind of mean, but all this talk about Max was really rubbing me the wrong way.

Ever since Monday I had been feeling like I was in some big competition with him — for the triathlon and for Sabs. Now I was more determined than ever for Sabrina and me to come in first of all the girls. That would show Max that *we* were good athletes without *his* help!

I knew Sabs wouldn't understand how I felt about Max, though, so I just dropped the subject. "Come on, let's do some curls with the leg weights now," I said, trying to act more enthusiastic than I felt. We still had to do our training, after all.

"Okay," Sabs agreed quietly. The way she looked at me made me feel kind of like I was the torture police or something.

While I was changing the weights, the door to the exercise room flew open and Michel, Sam, Nick, Arizonna, and Jason came bursting in.

Sam stopped dead in his tracks when he saw us. "Wow! Look at all the jocks in here! I don't think we're going to fit," he said sarcastically. Nick, Jason, Arizonna, and Michel stood next to him and laughed.

I couldn't believe it! Wasn't anyone going to take our training seriously? Why was everybody standing in the way of our getting in shape for this triathlon?

"Cut it out, guys!" I cried, getting really annoyed. "We're trying to work out!"

"I don't know why you're going so crazy, K.C.," Michel said earnestly. Sometimes he calls me by my nickname from the hockey team, K.C. It stands for Katie Campbell. "You could do that triathlon tomorrow and still do great," Michel went on to say.

I guess he was trying to pay me a compliment, but that still didn't change the fact that something was always ruining our training.

"That's not the point," I told him. "Everyone else who signed up could be just as good as me or better! I have to work really hard so I can beat everyone and win! I'd feel terrible if I didn't win just because I didn't train as hard as I could have!"

Everyone was staring at me, and I had to blink really fast to keep from crying.

"Maybe we should leave them alone, Michel. I wouldn't want to be accused of stopping Sabs from winning the triathlon!" Sam said with a big smirk on his face. Then he started laughing again. Nick, Jason, and Arizonna joined in, but Michel looked kind of embarrassed. I guess he could tell how upset I was.

"Come on, guys. We'll go swimming now and work out with the weights later," Michel offered.

Sabs, Katie, and Al were all looking at me expectantly. They didn't exactly look thrilled to be in the weight room anymore, so I told Michel, "No, that's okay. We're not getting much done in here anyway. You guys stay here, and we'll go swim. I want to show Sabs how to do a flip turn."

"Great, I love to swim," Sabs agreed.

I looked at her with relief as the four of us went to grab our towels from the hooks on the wall. Now maybe we could work out seriously!

"I just have to change into my suit and a bathing cap. The chlorine turns my hair funny colors. I'll be right down," Sabrina cried. She grabbed her workout bag and ran up the stairs to my bedroom to change.

I knew Sabrina could take half an hour to change her clothes. She and Al and Randy would have to leave before we could get much done. There was no way we were going to get to all the things on my schedule for today.

I sighed. Training for this triathlon just wasn't turning out the way I had planned at all.

Chapter Seven

"I can't believe the triathlon is this week-end!" I said when I got to our locker Wednesday morning, two weeks later.

Sabs had gotten to school ahead of me, and she was crouched down by her books at the bottom of the locker. "I know!" she exclaimed, looking up at me. "The IronKids Triathlon is only three days away!"

I was already starting to feel the kind of nervous anticipation that comes before a game. Sabs and I had been working out practically every day for almost three weeks now. I had to admit that she had gotten a little better. She could run and swim for longer than she could at first. And the weight training had helped give her more strength.

But somehow we never got nearly as much done as I'd planned. There were at least half a dozen things that hadn't gotten checked on my workout schedule.

I guess I should have been happy that we were making progress. But I still felt that I could use more time to train. I just knew that I wasn't working at my best pace, and that made me feel dissatisfied with myself. I knew it wasn't Sabs's fault, but she always managed to distract me somehow. I guess it's just because she's not as used to training as I am.

"We're working out at the sports complex today, right?" Sabrina asked, breaking into my thoughts.

"Mmm," I replied, feeling excited in spite of my worries. We planned to run through the whole course from start to finish, exactly the way we would do it during the triathlon. I had brought a stopwatch with me so we could get an idea of how long it would take.

"I can't wait!"

I grabbed the books for my first class, then gave Sabs a sidelong glance. She seemed a lot more enthusiastic about this than she had about any of the other stuff we'd been doing.

"Maybe Max will be there," she said. Standing on tiptoe, she looked at her reflection in the small mirror taped to the inside of our locker.

I should have known that was why she was so happy to be working out. "Well, even if he is, we're still going to run through the whole course," I said firmly.

"Okay," Sabrina said with a shrug.

"Did you bring everything we'll need?" I asked, trying not to sound too much like a nagging mother. It was just that I really didn't want any delays today.

Sabs tapped a large duffel bag that barely fitted in our locker. "All here!" she said.

"What's in there?" I asked, staring at the stuffed bag in disbelief.

"My bathing suit and cap, a towel, my running pants and a T-shirt, socks, a sweatshirt, a ponytail holder for the bike and running part, a brush, and sneakers," Sabrina listed. "Oh, and a hair dryer."

"Do you really think you're going to need all those things?" I asked.

She nodded her head emphatically. "Definitely. I have to dress differently for every event."

"Wait a minute," I said, shaking my head. "All you need is your bathing suit, and then your running pants to wear over it for the biking and running parts of the race. Sabs, if you change after the biking part, too, you'll lose too much time!"

"I don't think a few seconds will hurt," she said. "Besides, I'll do better if I'm happy with what I'm wearing."

Knowing Sabs, I thought that was probably true. Losing time when you didn't have to seemed crazy to me, but I decided not to tell her that. "What about your bike helmet? It's required for the triathlon," I reminded her.

Sabs made a face. "I know, but I don't want to wear it for practice. It looks weird and makes my hair flat."

"Your hair is going to be wet from the swimming anyway," I pointed out.

"That's what the bathing cap is for," Sabs said.

I just stood there staring at her. I had the feeling that we were actors on some kind of weird situation comedy, where no one seems to completely understand what the other person is talking about. But somehow, in our case, I didn't think this was funny.

***

"There he is!" Sabs whispered to me as we

walked out of the locker room and into the track area of the Acorn Falls Sports Complex.

I didn't have to ask who she was talking about. All day long I had been hoping that Max wouldn't be at the sports complex, but there he was. He was stretching on the rubberized surface surrounding the track, wearing these neon-orange workout clothes.

"Max, hi!" Sabrina called, waving to him.

Max flashed her a brilliant smile and waved back. Then he continued stretching.

"Um, Katie?" Sabs said, looking hesitantly at me. "Can we run first?"

I let out an angry sigh. Somehow I had known something like this would happen. Max was ruining everything!

"No!" I said. "We have to do the triathlon in the order we'll be doing it on Saturday. So that means we have to swim, then bike, and then run."

Sabs glanced over at Max again. "Well, I don't see any difference if we run first and then swim and bike," she said. "I mean, as long as we do all three eventually."

"Of course it makes a difference!" I said. "Why?"

I stuttered for a second, feeling really hurt that Sabs didn't trust me to be responsible for our training. "Because . . . because we have to change our shoes between events and . . . we have to get used to the order!"

Suddenly I couldn't think straight. I wasn't exactly sure why the order made a difference, but I was sure it did, and I wasn't going to change my mind for Max McAllister!

Sabs was looking down at the ground now, rubbing her sneaker toe against the rubber matting. "Well, how about you do it your way and I do it my way?" she suggested. "Then we can see if there is really a difference."

"Fine! Do whatever you want," I said hotly.

Sabs didn't even seem to notice that I was mad. She just said, "Great!" Then she ran over to the track and quickly stretched. She was stretching all wrong again, but obviously that didn't matter to her. She probably just wanted to get out on the track with Max, who had finished stretching and was already jogging.

If she doesn't want my help, then I'm sure not going to give it to her! I said to myself. Then I turned around and walked away really fast.

Tears stung my eyes, but I blinked them

back. I was really upset about the way Sabs was acting, but I tried to put it out of my mind and concentrate on getting in a good practice run-through.

I took a deep breath to calm myself. Then I went back to the front desk to get a bike to use. Once it was set up, I went to the pool and pulled off my warm-up clothes, so that I was just wearing my navy-blue tank suit.

I had gotten a waterproof stopwatch especially for this swim, and it was hanging around my neck by a string. After adjusting my goggles, I bent into a diver's crouch, pushed the button on my stopwatch, and began the 200-meter swim.

It felt really good to be in the water. As I counted off the laps, I mostly concentrated on doing good flip turns and pacing myself so that I wouldn't get too tired.

After the last lap, I pulled myself out of the water and ran to the pile of clothes I had waiting next to the pool. I threw my goggles and cap aside and quickly pulled on nylon exercise shorts, socks, sneakers, and my bicycle helmet. Then I sprinted to where I had left the bike and hopped on.

I was tempted to look at my stopwatch to see how long the swim had taken me, but instead I just concentrated on doing the laps on my bike without hitting any of the runners. With Max and Sabs and half a dozen other runners all over the place, it wasn't so easy. But I decided that I had better get used to distractions, since I wouldn't be alone on the track during the real triathlon.

The 6 miles on the bike seemed to go really fast. My muscles were already starting to shake when I dismounted, but I forced myself to keep going. Pulling off my helmet, I began to run the 1.2 miles.

I was starting to feel a little winded, but I tried to keep a fast pace through the run. Still, it seemed like forever before I was finally running the last half lap. I started to sprint then, giving it every ounce of energy I had left.

By the time I passed the white mark on the track, I was practically gasping for air. I was exhausted, and my heart felt like it was going to pound right out of my chest.

Somehow I managed to remember to hit the stopwatch to stop it. I breathed in huge gulps of air as I slowed to a walk. Then I realized that

Max and Sabs had stopped running and that Sabs was standing on the side, clapping for me.

"Katie, you were great!" she exclaimed, running over to me. "Gosh, I've never seen you run so fast! Aren't you tired?" she asked.

I nodded, still trying to catch my breath.

Max just stood there and didn't say anything to me.

I forced myself to walk around the track so my muscles could cool down slowly and wouldn't cramp up. Finally I was rested and could talk to Sabs. She and Max had finished running and were doing cool-down exercises now.

"How did I look?" I asked, plopping down next to Sabs.

"Great! If you do that Saturday, you'll definitely win," she told me.

I wasn't so sure about that, but it made me feel good to hear it anyway. I smiled at Sabs — until I saw the way Max was scowling. Ignoring him, I said to Sabrina, "Now you can run through, and I'll time you."

"That's okay, I don't want to run through it," Sabrina said casually.

For a moment I just stared at her. "What?

But that's the whole reason we came here!"

Sabs shrugged. "Well, Max says he's not going to run through the course. I don't think I have to, either. I mean, we practiced a lot already, and we ran three laps," Sabrina told me. "That's a mile and a half, which is more than we'll have to run in the race."

She glanced at her watch. "Anyway, Al and Randy said they were going to be at Fitzie's after they did some work at the library. Why don't we go meet them there instead."

I stared at her again, but then I just said, "Okay." I was way too exhausted to argue with her right then. But I promised myself that tomorrow we would work out without Max McAllister interfering.

Chapter Eight

"Hi, you guys," Randy greeted Sabs and me as she and Allison walked up to our locker Thursday morning.

"Just two days until the triathlon," Al added, smiling at us. "I can't wait to watch you."

"Really! You two must be totally psyched," Randy agreed.

"I can't wait!" Sabs said, nodding her head so that her red curls bounced around her face.

I turned and looked at her. How could she be so excited about a competition that she had no hope of winning? Even though she had worked out almost every day, she still hadn't trained according to our schedule. She hadn't even run through the course with me yesterday. She acted like she didn't even care about the race at all!

"Katie, aren't you excited?" Al asked, looking at me kind of funny. I guess she noticed I wasn't saying very much.

"Sure," I replied. I guess that was true, even if Sabs's attitude was really getting me down.

"You should have seen Katie yesterday on her practice run. She was great! She's definitely going to come in first of all the girls," Sabs said excitedly.

"Is that what Max said?" I asked. I guess it came out sounding kind of mean, but I was still feeling hurt about Sabs working out with Max yesterday instead of with me. I never thought that she would break our plans just because of a cute guy!

Sabs glanced at Randy and Al before answering my question. "Not exactly. But he did say he thought it was bad luck to run through the course before the race."

She was acting like it was a proven fact or something.

"Well, if Max says so, then it must be true," I said sarcastically.

Actually, I had a theory about Max. I thought part of the reason he spent so much time with Sabs was because she looked up to him. I even secretly thought he was being mean to me because he was afraid I was a better athlete than he was. But I didn't want to mention this to anyone.

Sabs frowned, looking at me. "Is something wrong, Katie?" she finally asked.

I took a deep breath and tried to calm down. "No," I told her. Then I changed the subject. "We're going to work out today after school, aren't we?"

Sabs looked like she wanted to say something. But then she just nodded. "Sure," she agreed. "What's the schedule for today?"

"We're running at the school's track. We'll do three miles there and then ride our bikes ten miles around town," I told her. I had originally planned to ride only six miles, but I added on a few more to make up for Sabs not doing anything yesterday except walk around the track with Max.

Sabrina frowned at me again. "Are you sure you want to do that much?" she asked.

"It is pretty cold out today," Randy added.

"It's not that cold out," I said. "We'll keep warm by moving. Just make sure you wear gloves and a hat, Sabs."

There was an unsure look in Sabs's eyes as

she said, "Um, Katie, I've never run three whole miles at once before. I've walked three miles, but never actually run them."

"Katie, do you really think you two should work out so hard so close to Saturday? I mean, you don't want to get sore or hurt or anything, right?" Al asked, looking concerned.

I just shrugged and said, "We have tomorrow to rest up for Saturday. We're only swimming and walking tomorrow."

I wasn't going to admit that today's workout was a little strenuous. I needed to know that I had tried as hard as I could to make sure Sabs and I could be the best on Saturday. Besides, running always helped me work out my frustrations.

"Well, I don't think Al and I will be joining you for this workout! I'm not ready for basic training, sir!" Randy joked, saluting me like I was an army general or something.

Al and Sabs started giggling, but I wasn't in a kidding-around mood at all.

"That's okay," I told Randy. "Sabs and I have to get a lot done today. We won't have any time to fool around with you guys."

"Um, okay," Al said slowly, looking out of

the corner of her eye at Randy.

Then the bell rang and we had to go to class. I guess what I had said hadn't sounded very nice, but I was just being honest. Training for a triathlon was serious business. Why couldn't anyone else understand that?

***

A few hours later Sabrina and I were chugging slowly around the school's track. I hit my gloved hands together to warm them. It really was pretty cold out, but I couldn't admit that to Sabs after I had made such a big deal out of saying that we'd be okay once we got moving.

"Four!" I said to myself as I finished my fourth lap. Slowing down, I turned around to see where Sabrina was. She had been lagging behind since the second lap.

"Come on, Sabs! Keep moving!" I yelled. I turned back around and ran in place until she caught up to me. She was breathing heavily and her face was red.

"How . . . many . . . more?" she managed to say between puffing breaths.

Bradley's track was only a quarter of a mile long, so we had to run twelve laps to make three miles. "Eight more laps," I told her. Then

I started running again.

A minute later I realized that Sabs had lagged behind again. I glanced over my shoulder — and then stopped completely. Turning around sharply, I stood there with my hands on my hips.

Sabs had stopped running! Now she was walking slowly and blowing on her mittens to warm her hands.

"Sabs!" I cried.

"Katie," she said, still trying to catch her breath. "I can't . . . run anymore!"

Then she just stopped and sat right down on the field.

"What are you doing? Get up!" I told her, running back to where she was sitting.

Sabs shook her head and looked up at me with this really stubborn expression on her face. "I can't. My side hurts and I'm cold and I don't want to run anymore."

"But we've barely gone a mile!" I argued. "The triathlon on Saturday is 1.2 miles! How do you expect to win if you can't even finish? Why did you even bother signing up for this?"

Then Sabs got to her feet and came over and stood right in front of me. "You're the one who wants to win!" she shouted angrily. "You're the one who is going to win! It's easy for you, Katie, you were born athletic! You do everything well! You get all A's in school, you're the star of the hockey team, and any guy you look at likes you! You're beautiful! You even live in a mansion with a millionaire! I can't compete with you, and I don't want to! So why are you forcing me to try and keep up with you!"

Tears had started trickling down Sabs's red face. Before I had a chance to say anything, she turned and ran off the field. She grabbed her bag, jumped on her bike, and was gone.

I just stood there in shock. An awful feeling was building up in my stomach, and I didn't know what to do about it.

Chapter Nine

Sabrina calls Randy.

RANDY: Yo!

SABRINA: *(Crying)* Randy?

RANDY: Sabs, is that you? What's wrong?

SABRINA: Katie and I had a big fight!

RANDY: About what? As if I have to ask.

SABRINA: What? What are you talking about?

RANDY: I just mean that there's been a lot of bad vibes between you two ever since this triathlon thing came up.

SABRINA: That's what we had the fight about! I couldn't run three miles today. I got a cramp in my side and I was cold and tired. I didn't see why we had to run three miles anyway. The running part of the triathlon is only 1.2 miles!

RANDY: Okay, calm down, Sabs. Just tell me what exactly you guys fought about.

SABRINA: Well, when I stopped running, Katie yelled at me. She said that I wasn't trying and why did I sign up in the first place.

RANDY: And then what?

(There is a pause.)

SABRINA: Then I yelled at her and told her it was easy for her because she's perfect and smart and pretty and rich.

RANDY: Sabs! You really said all that?

SABRINA: Yeah. And now I feel horrible about it! I don't know what to do, Randy. I'll just die if Katie never talks to me again. I just ran off the field and left her there.

RANDY: I'm sure she'll talk to you again. Don't worry. I mean, you two are really tight! It sounds like you both said some stuff you didn't mean.

SABRINA: I know! I didn't mean it, I swear!

RANDY: I know, Sabs.

SABRINA: What am I going to do?

RANDY: Just call her and tell her what you just told me.

SABRINA: I can't! What if she hates me?

RANDY: I'm sure she doesn't. But I'll tell you what. How about I call Katie and see what's up with her?

SABRINA: And then you can call me back and tell me if she's mad at me or not!

RANDY: Bingo!

SABRINA: Thanks, Ran. You're the best!

RANDY: Yeah, yeah, don't embarrass me, Sabs. Hang tough. I'll call you back in a few.

SABRINA: Okay, bye.

RANDY: *Ciao.*

Randy calls Allison.

MRS.
CLOUD: Hello?

RANDY: Hello, Mrs. Cloud! How are things? How's the new little bundle doing?

MRS.
CLOUD: (*Laughing*) Hello, Randy. The

	baby is just fine, thank you. Hold on, I'll get Allison.
ALLISON:	Hello?
RANDY:	Hey, Al. It's Randy. We've got problems.
ALLISON:	What's wrong?
RANDY:	Katie and Sabs had a blowout today at the track. Things are pretty tense.
ALLISON:	Oh, no. How did you find out?
RANDY:	Sabs just called me, all upset.
ALLISON:	What did they fight about?
RANDY:	The triathlon, what else!
ALLISON:	Yeah, I had a feeling things weren't going too well with their training together.
RANDY:	Me too. Anyway, Katie yelled at Sabs because she couldn't do three miles, and then Sabs totally lost it! She told Katie that it was easy for her since she's perfect!
ALLISON:	Oh, no! Katie has been a little too tough on Sabrina, though.
RANDY:	I know! I mean, Katie is used to really tough workouts from hockey. I guess she doesn't under-

	stand what it's like for the rest of us wimps!
ALLISON:	*(Laughing)* But we can't be too hard on Katie, either. She only wanted to make sure that Sabs does well in the race.
RANDY:	Yeah, especially since Sam was teasing Sabs so much. It would be pretty humiliating if Sabs couldn't finish or something after Katie and I made such a big deal about girls being as good athletes as boys. I guess we kind of screwed up.
ALLISON:	It did put a lot of pressure on Sabs. I think she joined the race because she thought it would be fun, not to be the best in Acorn Falls.
RANDY:	You're right, Al. I'm glad I called you. I'm supposed to call Katie and see if she's mad at Sabs and then call Sabs right back.
ALLISON:	Why don't I call Katie. I have a feeling I know what she's been going through, too.

RANDY: Would you? I have to cook dinner now. But call me later and tell me what's up, so I can talk to Sabs. *Ciao.*

ALLISON: Okay, bye.

Allison calls Katie.

MICHEL: *Bonjour!*

ALLISON: Hello, Michel. It's Allison. Is Katie there?

MICHEL: *Oui.* She just got out of the shower, but she doesn't look too happy. I'm keeping out of her way! Hold on. *(Sound of Michel yelling to Katie through the bathroom door.)*

KATIE: I got it, Michel. Hang up!

MICHEL: Chill out, eh? *(Michel hangs up loudly.)*

KATIE: Hello?

ALLISON: Hi, Katie. It's Allison.

KATIE: Hi, Al. I'm so glad you called! I did something terrible today.

ALLISON: What happened?

KATIE: I pushed Sabs really hard at the track. I practically called her lazy! I don't know why I did that. I know she can't run that fast for three miles straight.

ALLISON: You *have* been putting a lot of pressure on yourself and on Sabrina for the triathlon.

KATIE: I know. I feel really bad.

ALLISON: I think I know what the problem is. Sabs just signed up for the triathlon because she thought it would be fun. You know how she likes to be involved in things, and I'm sure she thought that working out with you would be . . . well, fun!

KATIE: And all I want to do is train all the time and win.

ALLISON: Exactly.

KATIE: Sabs probably hates me.

ALLISON: No, she doesn't, Katie. In fact, I bet she feels as bad as you do about today. You two were just on different wavelengths. Why don't you call her and talk things out?

KATIE: You're right, that's what I'll do right now! Oh — and, Al?

ALLISON: Yes?

KATIE: Thanks a lot. I really needed to talk about this.

ALLISON: No problem, Katie. See you tomorrow.

Katie calls Sabrina.

SABRINA: Randy?

KATIE: No, it's Katie.

SABRINA: Oh. Hi.

KATIE: Hi. *(She pauses.)* Sabs, I'm so sorry!

SABRINA: Oh, Katie! I'm sorry, too! I was so worried you were mad at me that I was afraid to call you!

KATIE: I thought you were mad at me!

(They both laugh.)

SABRINA: Katie, let's promise that we'll never fight again.

KATIE: Okay!

SABRINA: But my mom did tell me one thing when I told her about our fight.

KATIE: What?

SABRINA: She told me that we should talk about things so that they won't

	happen again.
KATIE:	That makes sense. But what are we supposed to talk about?
SABRINA:	About what made us mad at each other, so we understand how the other one felt.
KATIE:	Well, I think I understand what got you upset. I was pushing you too hard at our workouts. They weren't fun at all for you, but I just wanted to make sure that you and I came in first Saturday.
SABRINA:	But I don't want to come in first. I just want to finish. I don't even care if I come in in last place, as long as I know I did it. Besides, I wanted to do it to be with you. I thought it would be fun.
KATIE:	I'm sorry, Sabs. I didn't realize how you felt about finishing. I guess I thought that just because I wanted to win so badly, then you did, too.
SABRINA:	That's okay, Katie.
KATIE:	Well, that's not all of it. Don't forget I told Sam that you and I

were going to finish first! He's never going to let you forget it if you don't!

SABRINA: Don't worry about him. I mean, I don't think he could even finish the triathlon! At least I'm trying! Once I really do it, he won't dare make fun of me.

KATIE: I hope you're right, Sabs. I meant to tell you before. You really are doing well. I think you won't have a problem finishing if you just pace yourself. I guess I was mad that you acted like you wanted to be with Max Mc-Allister more than with me. And no offense, Sabs, but I don't like the way he treats me.

SABRINA: I noticed that! I don't know why, though. Everybody usually likes you! Anyway, I just thought that Max could help us, since he is a track star and all. He is cute, but I mostly hung out with him because he didn't make me work out so hard! You were practically killing me!

KATIE: *(Laughing)* Well, I didn't mean to. I'm sorry.

SABRINA: Me too. I didn't mean to hurt your feelings. So, can we still work out tomorrow?

KATIE: I think that you and I have trained enough already. If we're not ready now, we never will be. Besides, after today, I think our muscles could use a rest!

SABRINA: I know mine could use one! But are you sure, Katie? I mean, I know how important this race is to you.

KATIE: I'm sure.

SABRINA: Okay. Well, then, I'll meet you tomorrow at our locker before first period.

KATIE: Okay, bye.

SABRINA: Bye.

Chapter Ten

I woke up really early Saturday morning, feeling too excited to sleep anymore. Today was the IronKids Triathlon!

After my shower, I felt restless. On Saturday mornings my stepfather makes brunch if he's in town. But brunch wasn't for another hour, so I put on a heavy sweater, jeans, and boots and took a walk around our property. I figured that would help clear my mind and warm up my muscles. I walked around our pond and all the way to the edge of our property, where I could see the golf course of the Acorn Falls Country Club.

I felt a lot better about running the triathlon now that Sabs and I had straightened everything out. My mom told me that it's really important to respect the differences between people. Boy, I was learning that that was really true!

By the time I got back to the house, my cheeks were pink and my stomach was starting to growl. I walked in the back door and took off my boots in the mud room before I went into the kitchen.

Jean-Paul was at our big industrial stove cooking pancakes and sausages, and they smelled really good. My stomach started rumbling even louder. Looking at my watch, I saw that it was only nine-thirty. I figured that I could eat and still have time to digest my food before the triathlon at one o'clock.

It would only be a little while until brunch was ready, but I just couldn't stand around doing nothing. I ran upstairs to my room to do some more stretches. I was definitely going to need something to do every second until the triathlon started!

The minute I got up to my room, the Princess phone on my bedside table rang. I hurried over and picked it up.

"Hello?"

"Katie! I'm so excited I couldn't sleep!"

"Hi, Sabs," I said, laughing. "Me too."

"I don't know what I'm going to do until it's time to check in at the complex at twelve!"

Sabs's voice came back over the line.

"I know what you mean," I told her. "I already stretched and took a walk. I'll have to kill time until we have brunch, and then I guess I can get ready to go to the sports complex."

There was a pause before Sabs said, "Eat brunch? Are you sure that's okay?"

I nodded, as if Sabs could actually see me from all the way across town! "Sure," I said. "You have to eat something. I mean, you shouldn't eat right before the race, but now is okay."

"What are you having?" she asked.

I sat down on my bed and leaned against the pillows. "I guess pancakes, some fruit, orange juice, and maybe sausages. Why?" I asked.

"Well, I read somewhere that you're supposed to eat spaghetti before a race. But I don't know if I could eat that for breakfast."

I couldn't help laughing. "Sabs, you don't have to eat spaghetti! You can have any kind of high-carbohydrate food before a race, for energy. Actually, I think you're supposed to eat some the night before."

"Oh, no! Now it's too late! We had pizza last

night for dinner!" Sabs cried, horrified.

"Don't worry, Sabs. I think pizza must have some carbohydrates in it," I assured her.

I could hear her sigh of relief. "Oh, good! Anyway, I called to see what you're going to wear for the triathlon."

"I guess what I wore for my practice run. You know, my tank suit, nylon shorts, running shoes, and socks."

"No — I meant, what are you wearing to the triathlon," she corrected herself.

I laughed. It figured that Sabs would be most concerned with that! "I'm going to put a pair of sweatpants and my triathlon T-shirt over my bathing suit. And then a sweatshirt," I said. "What are you going to wear?"

"My new purple-and-yellow running pants over my blue bathing suit, and then my tie-dyed yellow, blue, and purple socks and my triathlon T-shirt," Sabs said in one big rush. "Mark is even letting me borrow his yellow zip-up sweatshirt."

"That sounds really great, Sabs," I told her.

"Thanks! Well, I better go eat now before it gets too late," Sabs said. "I'll see you at the sports complex at twelve. I hope Al and Randy get there early, too, so they can get a good seat!"

"See you soon!" I said, starting to get really excited. Then I thought of something. "Sabs?"

"Yes?"

"I'm really glad we entered together," I told her.

"Me too!" she answered. "See you in a little while."

"Bye."

After I hung up, I sat there on my bed, smiling to myself. I was more psyched now for the triathlon than ever!

Chapter Eleven

A few hours later Sabs and I were both at the sports complex standing in a crowd of contestants. It seemed like the whole track and swimming area was packed. After three weeks of training and waiting, this was it!

The Seniors group was racing first. Because there were so many of us, we were racing in teams. There were three teams in all, and the second group had just started swimming their laps. Sabs and I were in the third group. The crowd in the bleachers cheered like crazy, while the last ten Seniors racers warmed up on the sidelines of the track. The Juniors were all crowded in with us, watching and waiting until it was their turn.

"Stay still, Sabs," I said. "I have to clip your number on." Sabs was jumping around a lot from being so excited. Not that I could blame her. I couldn't stand still myself.

Suddenly she turned around and looked at the plastic-covered number I was holding, and her face fell. "Number twenty-four? I don't want that number!" she protested.

"Why not!" I asked.

"Because it's not a lucky number for me!" she replied, looking horrified.

One thing about Sabs is that she's very superstitious. I knew she wouldn't be happy until she got a number that she thought was lucky.

I didn't think it would be easy to get her another one, though. The organizers of the triathlon had set up a special desk where they gave out numbers to the contestants. They had a list that showed which kid had which number, so they could know who the winners were. I didn't know if they had any numbers to spare.

"Well, maybe you can just take my number," I suggested hopefully.

"No, your number isn't lucky, either!" she cried. Then her hands flew to her mouth. "Oh! I didn't mean that it won't be lucky for you. It's just that it's not lucky for me," she explained quickly.

Smiling at her, I said, "It's okay, Sabs. I understand."

I looked down at my own white plastic square with the number seven on it. Actually, seven had been my father's lucky number when he played semi-pro hockey. I kind of felt like it would bring me luck, too. Having his number made me wish he was still alive to see me compete in today's race.

"What am I going to do?" Sabs asked, bringing me back to earth.

"Well, let's figure this out systematically," I suggested. "What number is lucky for you?"

"Thirteen," she answered right away.

I gave her a curious look. "But, Sabs, most people are terrified of the number thirteen! My mom even told me that they usually don't have a row number thirteen in airplanes."

"Well, that's dumb," she said. "I mean, even if they don't call it row number thirteen, it still is, if you count!"

Looking at the second group of racers, I saw that most of them were biking now. I figured we still had maybe half an hour before our group would start. "Okay, let's see if they still have number thirteen at the triathlon desk," I said.

Our bags with all our equipment and clothes were on the ground next to us. We picked them up and we started back toward the desk where the officials were. I was really glad we had arrived extra early. Getting ready for the race was taking longer than I had thought it would, but I didn't really mind. At least it took my mind off how nervous I was feeling!

"Katie! Sabs!" I heard Randy's voice above the cheers.

Looking around, I saw them in the bleachers in an area that had been a cordoned-off. All of the the spectators had to stay behind those ropes. Al and Randy were both holding red banners that said GO KATIE! on one side and GO SABRINA! on the other. Sabrina and I walked over to the area and stood by the ropes.

"Hi, guys!" I called out loudly, waving at them.

"Those banners are fantastic! Thanks!" Sabs called.

"How are you two doing?" Al asked. She and Randy had come down the bleacher steps to stand by us. "Can we help you with anything?"

"Actually, you can," I said. "We need to ask the officials if Sabs can trade in her number for number thirteen," I told them. "That's her lucky number."

"I have to have it!" Sabs added.

Randy raised her eyebrows and nodded. "No problemo. Al and I can take care of that." Then she said softly to Al, "I think Katie worked Sabs so hard that she lost her marbles!"

"I heard that!" I said, pretending to be mad.

"Just kidding, Katie. We'll be right back," Randy said. Then she and Allison were off.

The arena was getting pretty warm with all the people crowding into it, so I took off my warm-up sweatshirt. When I turned around to put it in my nylon bag, I was facing Michel, Sam, Nick, Arizonna, and Jason. They were standing right where Al and Randy had just been.

"Hi, guys!" I said, smiling at them.

"Hi!" Sabs chimed in. She looked at Sam to see if he was going to tease her. But luckily he was busy talking to some other kids from school. All he did was kind of wave to us.

"Wow, look at all these people!" Nick said, looking around.

I had to admit that I hadn't expected there to be so many spectators, or so many kids entered. There were a lot more boys, though, than there were girls. An illuminated scoreboard showed the best times so far for the girls and boys. My practice time was about a minute better than the girls' time, but I was still worried. I had spotted a few girls that I recognized from Bradley's track team. They were warming up, which meant that they would be in the same group as Sabs and me. With them competing against me, this definitely wasn't going to be an easy race to win!

"Hi, K.C.," Michel said, bringing my attention back to him and the other guys. "Mom, Dad, and Emily said to tell you they're up there," he added, pointing.

I looked up at the stands until I found Mom, Emily, and Jean-Paul. I waved at them, and they all waved back and cheered.

"Come here a second, K.C.," Michel continued, turning away from the other guys. I went over to him, and he said, "I brought you my lucky rabbit's foot for luck. If you rub it and make a wish, it will come true."

I was really surprised to hear him say that. I mean, I hadn't known before that Michel was superstitious. I thought it was really nice of him to bring me the rabbit's foot.

"Thanks," I told him, smiling. Then I closed my eyes, made a wish, and rubbed the soft rabbit's fur.

When I opened my eyes, I realized that the second group of racers were all running now. Pretty soon our group would start the competition! Randy and Al were nowhere in sight, but I decided not to worry about them. They would find us somehow.

The other contestants in the third Seniors group were all stretching and warming up. There were six guys and two other girls besides Sabs and me. Max was there, doing his leg kicks. When he saw Sabs, he grinned at her and gave her a thumbs-up. He looked pretty sure that he would win.

"Come on, Sabs. We better start stretching," I told her.

Sabs looked worriedly around. "What about my number?" she asked.

"You'll have to use this one for now, just in case Randy and Al can't find thirteen," I told her.

"I guess so," Sabrina cried, not happy.

I clipped the number on the back of her suit, and she put mine on. Then we sat on the ground and began to stretch. It was hard to get anything done with the race going on. I couldn't resist watching a little.

Suddenly the clapping got louder as the first runners crossed the finish line. I looked up at the scoreboard anxiously. Now the best girls' time was just five seconds slower than my practice time!

Before I knew it, a whistle was blowing and a voice over the loudspeaker told all the spectators to quiet down.

"I guess it's time!" I told Sabs. I was really getting butterflies in my stomach now.

Sabs was still scanning the crowd for Randy and Allison when a voice said over the loudspeaker system, "Athletes in the Seniors Group Number Three, please take your starting places!"

"We can't worry about the number now, Sabs," I said. I quickly pulled off my sweatpants, then bounced anxiously on the balls of my feet.

"A reminder to the contestants," the amplified voice went on. "There is no running between the events. You must walk between the pool, the bikes, and the track!"

That made me even more nervous. I hadn't even thought about that while I was training. I hoped I would remember not to run so I wouldn't be disqualified!

Sabs and I went together to the end of the pool and placed our shorts, sneakers, and socks where we could grab them as soon as we finished the swimming. Then we made sure our bikes were where we had left them by the track. Mine was standing up and ready with my helmet on the seat.

Finally we joined the other racers at the pool. I was just about to pull my swim goggles over my eyes when Randy and Al came running up.

"We got it!" they cried, holding up a plastic card with "13" printed on it.

"Where were you guys?" Sabs asked while Al clipped the number on her suit, removing the other one.

"Sorry it took us so long, but we got recruited," Randy said.

"What?" I asked, looking at her in confusion.

Al nodded. "The judges asked us if we would be lap counters. We have to pick one contestant and count how many laps they do in the pool and around the track."

"Swimmers, take your marks!" the voice said.

Hearing that, my breath caught in my throat. "We have to go!" I said, heading for my block while Sabs took her place two blocks down. Swimmers stand on raised blocks of wood, when making a dive, to keep from slipping on the edge of the pool.

Suddenly I thought of something. "Who's my counter?" I called back to Randy and Al.

Allison grinned and pointed to herself. "I am!"

The next few seconds were a complete blur. All I know is that I heard the gun and somehow managed to dive into the cool water. The lanes seemed close, probably because there were ten swimmers in the water at once. I tried to block the others out as I concentrated on making perfect flip turns and keeping even strokes in my freestyle swimming.

I still felt pretty good when I finished the last lap. As soon as I pulled my head up out of the water, I saw Allison's familiar face.

"You're done! Go!" she cried excitedly.

I pulled myself out of the water and onto the deck. As I whipped off my goggles and cap, I caught a glimpse of Sabrina still in the water. She was swimming freestyle with her head way out of the water and it was hurting her time.

As quickly as I could, I pulled my shorts onto my wet body and put on my socks and sneakers. I noticed that most of the boys were already out of the water and on their bikes — including Max.

I was careful to walk over to my bike. Then I put my helmet on and took off. I tried to keep track, in my head, of how many laps I had completed, but after the first four or so, I lost count. Luckily, Al was always standing right there when I finished each lap, and she held up her fingers to show me how many I had done.

I was in front of all the girls, but there were

some guys in front of me. I rode in close behind one of them so there would be less wind resistance. That's called drafting, which is something I had seen professional bike riders do on TV. Now that I'd tried it myself, I saw it really worked!

I finished the bike part ahead of the girls and only behind a few of the guys. I wanted to see how Sabs was doing, but I just couldn't get a good look.

Now came the hard part. The other two girls were on the track team, so I knew I would have problems keeping my lead. Without wasting a second, I dropped my bike, threw my helmet off to the side, and started running.

The running part of the race was just a little more than two times around the huge track. In the first lap, I paced myself and tried not to go too fast. As I started on my second lap, I thought I saw a purple-and-yellow blur of color out of the corner of my eye. I knew that had to be Sabs.

"Katie, you have a little more than a lap to go!" Al called to me.

Looking ahead, I saw that I was behind the other two girls, but not too far behind. I had paced myself so I was fairly close to them, but I had also saved enough energy to pour on some speed during the end of the last lap. I could tell that the girl in the lead was really confident that she had it won. She wasn't even running at full speed.

Then I made my move. I began to run a little faster and passed the girl in second. Then, when the finish line was in sight, I clenched my teeth and ran as fast as I could.

I was concentrating so hard that I didn't even know if I had won until Allison came running up to me at the finish line and hugged me.

"You did it! You won!" she cried.

"I . . . did?" I cried, out of breath.

"Well, four of the boys came in first, but you came in in first place for the girls," she told me. Then she handed me a plastic bottle of water, most of which I poured over my hot face.

I looked up at the scoreboard and saw a time that was thirty seconds better than my trial time. Listed next to it was number seven — my number.

"What . . . about . . . Sabs?" I asked, bending over to catch my breath.

Al pointed back to the track. "She's still out

there! Randy is her counter. I think she has a lap left."

"That's half a mile!" I cried. As I glanced at the track, I saw that all of the other runners were already in. Even the audience was beginning to come out of the bleachers to congratulate the contestants.

I felt horrible. Sabs was going to finish the race and no one would be there to congratulate her! I had to do something.

"I have to go help her!" I told Al. Then I jogged out to where Sabrina was rounding a turn.

"Katie! What . . . are you . . . doing?" she managed to say as I started running with her. She was running really slowly and breathing heavily. She looked just about out of breath. From the way she was holding her side, I could tell she had a cramp, too.

"Take deep, slow breaths, and your cramp will feel better," I told her.

She nodded and tried to do what I said.

"Only one more lap to go!" I urged.

Sabs started to falter, and I knew she was exhausted. But she still didn't give up. I was really proud of her. This race was so hard for her, but she had tried and she was going to finish. That was a huge accomplishment for her — I didn't care what Sam or Max or anybody said!

"You can do it. Just keep a slow, steady pace and concentrate on something," I instructed.

"On what?" she huffed.

"How about . . . the number thirteen!" I suggested.

That at least made Sabs smile. Pretty soon we were passing Randy, who jumped up and down and ran alongside of us. "You're almost done, Sabs!" she cried.

I could see the finish line up ahead. Most of the racers in our groups had cleared away, but there were still some athletes who hadn't gone to the locker room to change. And the kids in the Juniors group were all watching and cheering for Sabs.

When we crossed the line, Randy and Al were both jumping up and down, cheering. Sabs started to collapse to the ground, but I grabbed her arm and wouldn't let her. "You have to keep walking around or your muscles will cramp up."

She let out a groan, but let me lead her around. Then, all of the sudden, she looked up at me and said, "You won, didn't you?"

I smiled. "Yeah!"

"Congratulations! I knew you could do it!" she said breathlessly.

"And I knew *you* could do it!" I cried, hugging her.

She wrinkled her nose. "I came in last. Actually, I came in even worse than last," she said, gesturing to some athletes who were standing around in fresh clothes. "I came in after everyone else had showered and changed! So much for lucky thirteen!"

"Sabs! Don't you say that. You finished. That's what's important, and I'm really proud of you!" I cried.

Just then I noticed Max walking over to where everyone had left their bikes. He was dressed in jeans and a button-down shirt and he didn't look very happy.

"Hi, Max," Sabs called, waving to him. "How did you do?"

"Second," he answered curtly. He didn't even bother to come over to us.

"Wow. Well, Katie came in first for the

girls," Sabrina went on.

Max paused to scowl at us. Then he got his bike and walked away.

Sabs and I looked at each other and started cracking up. "So much for all of his bragging," Sabs said. "I guess his theories about training weren't so great after all!"

She hugged me, and then Randy and Allison jumped in and hugged us both.

"You guys are both winners!" Allison cried.

"Hey, Sabs," a boy's voice said behind us.

We all turned to see Sam standing there, looking uncomfortable. The other guys were standing in a group by the bleachers, watching.

"Hi, Sam," Sabs said.

He just looked at her for a moment. Then he grinned and said, "Nice race, Sabs. I really mean it. You too, Katie."

Sabs looked at me and smiled. I smiled back, and we both said in unison, "Thanks!"

Don't Miss
GIRL TALK #36
SABRINA AND THE CALF-RAISING
DISASTER

After lunch most of the other kids decided to bob for apples. But Randy wanted a tour of the farm. I had to admit, I was a little curious, too. I didn't know how a farm worked. It was interesting to see all the different machines and buildings as Jason pointed them out.

"Do you want to see the calf I'm raising for the 4-H Fair." said Jason.

"That sounds great," I agreed. I'd never seen a live calf up close.

We went outside to a small fenced-in pen. There were two four-legged black-and-white animals roaming around. Jason pointed to one. "That's her," he said proudly. "Her name's Army."

I couldn't think of a thing to say. It was the first calf I'd ever seen up close in my whole life. "She's pretty," I said finally. She was, too. She had big splotches of black and white all over her body.

Jason looked at her proudly. "I've been working with her every day, teaching her to lead."

"What's that?" I asked.

"You have to teach the calf to walk around and stand and sit with a rope around its neck," Jason explained. "It's one of the competitions for calves at the fair. I'm hoping I can win this year."

He couldn't seem to take his eyes off his calf, but I got a little bored looking at her. After a moment I looked over at the other calf, the one he hadn't said anything about. "Who's that?" I asked.

Jason glanced over. "Oh, that's the other one," he shrugged. "I'm not planning to enter her in the competition."

"Doesn't she even have a name?" I asked. I couldn't help thinking the poor little thing looked awfully cute. She gave me a kind of fast look out of her big brown eyes. Then she dipped her head down and looked at her hoofs, like she was really shy. After a second she looked up again. I could swear she was actually winking at me!

TALK BACK!
TELL US WHAT YOU THINK ABOUT
GIRL TALK BOOKS

Name _____

Address _____

City _____ State _____ Zip_____

Birthday _____ Mo._____ Year _____

Telephone Number (____)_____

1) Did you like this GIRL TALK book?

Check one: YES_____ NO_____

2) Would you buy another Girl Talk book?

Check one: YES_____ NO_____

If you like GIRL TALK books, please answer questions 3-5;
otherwise, go directly to question 6.

3) What do you like most about GIRL TALK books?

Check one: Characters_____ Situations_____
            Telephone Talk_____Other_____

4) Who is your favorite GIRL TALK character?

Check one: Sabrina_____ Katie_____ Randy_____
Allison_____ Stacy_____ Other (give name) _____

5) Who is your *least* favorite character?

_____

6) Where did you buy this GIRL TALK book?

Check one: Bookstore____Toy store____Discount store____
Grocery store___Supermarket___Other (give name)_____

Please turn over to continue survey.

7) How many GIRL TALK books have you read?

Check one: 0_____   1 to 2_____   3 to 4 _____   5 or more_____

8) In what type of store would you look for GIRL TALK books?

Bookstore_____Toy store_____Discount store_____

Grocery store_____Supermarket_____Other (give name)_____

9) Which type of store would you visit most often if you wanted to buy a GIRL TALK book?

Check *only* one: Bookstore_____Toy store_____

Discount store_____Grocery store_____Supermarket_____

Other (give name)_____

10) How many books do you read in a month?

Check one: 0_____   1 to 2_____   3 to 4 _____   5 or more_____

11) Do you read any of these books?

Check those you have read:

The Babysitters Club_____   Nancy Drew_____

Pen Pals_____   Sweet Valley High _____

Sweet Valley Twins_____Gymnasts_____

12) Where do you shop most often to buy these books?

Check one: Bookstore_____Toy store_____

Discount store_____Grocery store_____Supermarket_____

Other (give name)_____

13) What other kinds of books do you read most often?

_____

14) What would you like to read more about in GIRL TALK?

_____

_____

Send completed form to :

GIRL TALK Survey #3, Western Publishing Company, Inc.

1220 Mound Avenue, Mail Station #85

Racine, Wisconsin 53404

LOOK FOR THE AWESOME GIRL TALK BOOKS IN A STORE NEAR YOU!

HERE ARE MORE GIRL TALK TITLES TO LOOK FOR:

#31 IT'S A SCREAM!
#32 KATIE'S CLOSE CALL
#33 RANDY AND THE PERFECT BOY
#34 SHAPE UP, ALLISON!

Also look for these Nonfiction titles:
ASK ALLIE: 101 answers to your questions about boys, friends, family, and school!

YOUR PERSONALITY QUIZ: Fun, easy quizzes to help you discover the real you!